Dinner with Dracula

A Spine-Tingling Collection of Frighteningly Funny Poems

Edited by

Bruce Lansky

"The King of Giggle Poetry"

Illustrated by Mike and Carl Gordon

M Meadowbrook Press

Distributed by Simon & Schuster
New York

Contents

Advice from Dracula

Don't ever dine with Frankenstein;
he feasts on flaming turpentine.
He chomps and chews on soles of shoes
and quaffs down quarts of oily ooze.
At suppertime he'll slurp some slime.
He's known to gnaw on gristly grime.
His meals of mud and crispy crud
will curl your hair and chill your blood.
His poison, pungent, putrid snacks
may cause you seizures and attacks.
Your hair may turn completely white.
You may pass out or scream in fright.
Your skin will crawl.
Your throat will burn.
Your eyes will bulge.
Your guts will churn.
Your teeth will clench.
Your knees will shake.
Your hands will sweat.
Your brain will bake.
You'll cringe and cry.
You'll moan and whine.
You'll feel a chill
run down your spine.
You'll lose your lunch.
You'll lose your head.
So come...
and dine with me instead.

I Thought I Saw a Ghost Last Night

I thought I saw a ghost last night—
a goblin or a ghoul,
an ugly little creature
oozing salivary drool.

It had an eerie figure
and a huge gigantic nose.
It wasn't wearing sneakers
and was minus all its clothes.

It hovered through my bedroom
as I tried to catch some z's.
It appeared to have a lesion
or a facial skin disease.

I rubbed the sleep from both my eyes
and loomed a little nearer.
I knew what I had seen
was just my image in the mirror.

Paul R. Orshoski

The Creature in the Classroom

It appeared inside our classroom
at a quarter after ten,
it gobbled up the blackboard,
three erasers and a pen.
It gobbled teacher's apple
and it bopped her with the core.
"How dare you!" she responded.
"You must leave us...there's the door."

The Creature didn't listen
but described an arabesque
as it gobbled all her pencils,
seven notebooks and her desk.
Teacher stated very calmly,
"Sir! You simply cannot stay,
I'll report you to the principal
unless you go away!"

But the thing continued eating,
it ate paper, swallowed ink,
as it gobbled up our homework
I believe I saw it wink.
Teacher finally lost her temper.
"OUT!" she shouted at the creature.
The creature hopped beside her
And GLOPP...it gobbled teacher.

Jack Prelutsky

Under the Bed

There's a terrible green monster
    who lives beneath my bed.
I hear his long white teeth click.
    He's waiting to be fed.
I shiver underneath my sheets
    and squeeze my eyes up tight.

Maybe if I lie real still
    he won't eat me tonight…
He taps me on the shoulder.
    I don't know what to do.
He looks at me and says, "I'm scared!
    Can I get in with you?"

Penny Trzynka

Fraidy Cat

Every night he wakes me up,
all crying and upset.
He thinks he heard a monster,
and now his bed is wet.

"I heard a noise, and now I'm scared,"
he says through all the tears.
I wipe his face and pat his head
and hug away his fears.

I check for ghosts inside his room
and look behind the door.
I scare off all the bogeymen
and tell him, "Cry no more."

I understand his fear of ghosts.
It wouldn't be so bad,
but it's really kind of silly—
this fraidy cat's my dad.

Matthew M. Fredericks

9

Which Witch?

There once was a mean, ugly witch
who with her twin sister would switch.
So just like the other
not even their mother
could figure out which witch was which.

Linda Knaus

Bigfoot's Bottom

While roaming through the wilderness
one daunting, creepy night,
I noticed a mysterious,
spine-tingling, shocking sight.

Through fog and mist I slithered through
the haunted atmosphere,
and right there in the ground I saw
a print of Bigfoot's rear.

Though scientists have searched to find
where ape-men placed their feet,
I just might be the first to find
where Bigfoot took a seat.

Paul R. Orshoski

My Gramps and I Are Werewolves!

My grandpa is a werewolf,
and he thinks that no one knows.
But every time the moon is full
his hairy body grows.
His teeth turn into scary fangs.
He grows enormous ears.
He turns into a monstrous thing
that everybody fears.
He yowls and howls and makes such noise
the neighbors lock their doors.
I think that I'm the only one
who loves it when he roars.
Then last month when it happened
I began to howl, too.
And all the neighbors thought
that they were living near a zoo.
But howling's not the only thing
that happened on that night.
My ears turned long and pointy,
and I grew a tail of white.
And then my nose grew very long.
My ears began to shiver.
Then my feet turned into paws.
My jaw began to quiver.
I ran into the bathroom,
and I saw a gruesome sight.
I'd turned into a werewolf
like my grandpa on that night!
Now Gramps and I can't wait each month
to prowl the neighborhood,
and when the moon is full
on Halloween it's extra good!
We chase the trick-or-treaters,
and we make them run away.
I wish that full moon Halloween
would happen every day!

Kathy Kenney-Marshall

Scary Costume

With an evil eye that stares you down
and a bulbous warty nose,
a furrowed brow, a nasty scowl,
and old outdated clothes,
my costume is the scariest
the world has ever seen.
I'm not an ogre, ghost, or ghoul:
I'm a teacher for Halloween.

Robert Pottle

13

The Fall-Apart Monster

"Pardon me, Professor," said the creature as he trembled.
"There seems to be a problem in the way I've been assembled.
I like my head and body, and my pieces seem to fit.
I only think you may have rushed the job a little bit.

"It's pretty clear I am not built as well as I could be.
This morning I had seven toes, but now I'm down to three.
I clatter when I'm burping, and I rattle when I speak.
I try to hum and whistle, but I only grunt and squeak.

"I think my ears are inside out. My mouth is upside down.
I hear the things I think about, and when I smile, I frown.
I have no bellybutton, and I think you will agree
my feet are pointing backward, and that really shouldn't be.

"I see that you are eating, so I'll wait and understand,
but after you have finished, I could really use a hand."
"I'll give a hand," the doctor said, "but, buddy, here's the scoop:
You'll need another nose as well—it just fell in my soup!"

Eric Ode

14

Science Homework

I hope that you believe me,
for I wouldn't tell a lie.
I cannot turn my science homework in
and this is why:

I messed up the assignment
that you gave us yesterday.
It burbled from its test tube
and went slithering away.

It wriggled off the table,
and it landed with a splat,
convulsed across my bedroom floor
and terrorized the cat.

It shambled down the staircase
with a horrid glorping noise.
It wobbled to the family room
and gobbled all my toys.

It tumbled to the kitchen
and digested every plate.
That slimy blob enlarged
with every item that it ate.

It writhed around the living room,
digesting lamps and chairs,
then snuck up on our napping dog
and caught him unawares.

I came to school upset today.
My head's in such a fog.
But this is my excuse:
You see, my homework ate my dog.

Kenn Nesbitt

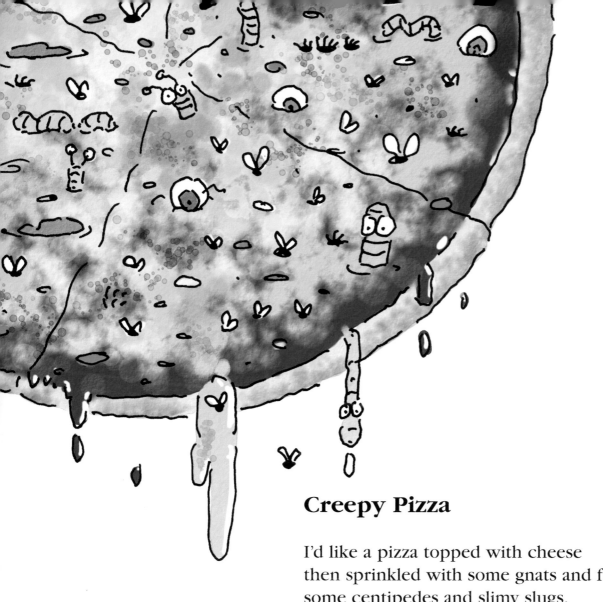

Creepy Pizza

I'd like a pizza topped with cheese
then sprinkled with some gnats and fleas,
some centipedes and slimy slugs,
and other creepy, crawly bugs.

I want to add some fingernails
and oyster ooze and crunchy snails
and chicken bones and spoiled meat
and smelly socks from dirty feet.

I want it topped with lots of mold
and gooey boogers (not too old),
a lot of snot, a little spit,
and guts with grimy, grainy grit.

I want the most disgusting crust
with spider webs and day-old dust
and dirt and mud and blood and gore
delivered to my sister's door.

Neal Levin

The Two-Headed Monster

A two-headed monster
broke into my house.
He ate every button
on Jennifer's blouse.

He tasted a table
and chewed on a bed.
He swallowed the hat
on my grandfather's head.

The monster ingested
the living room floor.
He scarfed down a painting
and dined on a door.

He snacked on the sofa.
He munched on the mats.
He sampled the fur
on my kittens and cats.

Although he enjoyed
all the things that he ate,
he suffered a tragic,
unfortunate fate.

The doctors confirmed it.
I heard what they said.
He ate mother's cooking,
and now he is dead.

Darren Sardelli

17

Sweet Dreams

It's always been a wish of mine
(or should I say a dream)
to scare my sister half to death
and hear her piercing scream.

That's why I squished four bugs until
they all were very dead,
then took them to my sister's room
and put them in her bed.

After we had said goodnight
my heart began to pound.
I waited and I waited, but
she never made a sound.

And then I got so doggone tired
I couldn't stay awake.
I climbed into my own warm bed
and shrieked—there was a snake!

It wiggled, and I leaped and fell
and bruised my bottom half.
Then I heard an awful sound—
it was my sister's laugh.

Joyce Armor

Vampire Brat

On the night he was bit by a vampire bat,
my brother turned into a vampire brat.
He used to be someone I tried to ignore,
but now he's obnoxious like never before.

He brushes his teeth, then he sharpens his fangs.
He sweeps back his hair to get rid of his bangs.
He swoops through the room, and he messes my hair.
He's weird. I mean, look how he dresses, I swear.

He says I've got zits, such an ugly complexion,
but look in the mirror—he's got no reflection.
At dinner he makes me feel very uptight
when he raises his eyebrows and asks for a "bite."

He stays up all night watching movies and junk,
then he sleeps upside down from the top of his bunk.
My friends won't come over. My life is a wreck.
Let's face it, my brother's a pain in the neck.

Neal Levin

20

The Creature

In the middle of the night,
in the part that's known as "dead,"
I wake and hear the breathing
of the creature 'neath my bed.

Sometimes he growls and threatens me,
sometimes he only stares.
He's big and mean and ugly,
and I shiver when he glares.

His B. O. fills the bedroom,
and his breath is awful, too.
His teeth are caked with ick and grime;
he should be in a zoo.

Instead, he lives beneath me—
it's like rooming with a skunk.
The creature's my big brother,
and he has the lower bunk.

Bill Dodds

Tinkle, Tinkle, Little Bat

Tinkle, tinkle, little bat,
wonder where the potty's at?

Straight ahead or to the right?
Caves are very dark at night.

Little bat, why do you frown?
Did you tinkle upside down?

Dianne Rowley

Frankenstein's Walk

He always walks with arms straight out,
his legs as stiff as can be.
Some say that makes him scary,
but it doesn't frighten me.

My baby brother walks that way
when he's not being hyper.
His straight-leg waddle simply means
he's loaded up his diaper.

Bill Dodds

Mama Monster's Lullaby

Sweet wee baby,
go to sleep.
Count your warts
instead of sheep.

Close your fiery
red-rimmed eyes,
and hush your moaning,
shrieking cries.

Snore and snuffle,
pick your nose.
It's okay, babe,
to suck your toes.

Chew your favorite
squeaky toy.
Goodnight, sleep tight,
my monster boy.

Marilyn Helmer

23

Frankenswine

At midnight Dr. Frankenswine
was in his lab, awake and fine.
He cackled queerly and began
describing his outlandish plan:

"The time has come to build a beast
from parts of pigs all now deceased
and processed foods from butchered hogs,
like sausage links and red hot dogs."

He slapped together bacon meat,
bologna, wieners, pickled feet,
and added headcheese, ribs, and ham
and patched it up with lots of Spam.

"My pet," said Dr. Frankenswine,
"awaken—hope you're feeling fine."
He zapped this creature of the grave
with power from the microwave.

The creature rose from life support.
He yawned and then he gave a snort.
He said, "There must be something more.
If this is life, then life's a boar."

The doctor cried out in defeat,
"You selfish brat! You're spoiled meat!
And so," said Dr. Frankenswine,
"I guess I'll take a break and dine."

He took a shiny, silver fork
and stabbed the monster made of pork.
He carved him up and took a bite
and licked his chops with pure delight.

The doctor turned that filthy beast
into a most delicious feast
and then declared when he was through,
"I made a pig of myself, too."

Neal Levin

25

Hey, Ma, Something's under My Bed

I hear it at night
when I turn out the light.
It's that creature who's under my bed.
He won't go away.
He's determined to stay.
But I wish he would beat it, instead.

I told him to go,
but he shook his head no.
He was worse than an unwelcome guest.
I gave him a nudge,
but he still wouldn't budge.
It was hard to get rid of the pest.

So I fired one hundred
round cannonballs plundered
from pirate ships sailing the seas.
But he caught them barehanded
and quickly grandstanded
by juggling them nice as you please.

The creature was slick.
He was clever and quick.
This called for a drastic maneuver.
So I lifted my spread
and charged under the bed
with the roar of my mother's new Hoover.

But he snorted his nose
and sucked in the long hose,
the canister, cord, and the plug,
and vacuumed in dust
till I thought he would bust
then he blew it all over the rug.

Now this made me sore,
so I cried, "This is war!"
and sent in a contingent of fleas,
an army of ants
dressed in camouflage pants,
followed closely by big killer bees.
But he welcomed them in
with a sly, crafty grin,
and he ate them with crackers and cheese.

I screamed, "That's enough!"
It was time to get tough.
"You asked for it, Creature," I said,
as I picked up and threw,
with an aim sure and true,
my gym sneaker under the bed.

With each whiff of the sneaker
the creature grew weaker.
He staggered out gasping for air.
He coughed and he sneezed
and collapsed with a wheeze
and accused me of not playing fair.

Then holding his nose
with his twelve hairy toes,
the creature curled into a ball,
and rolled 'cross the floor
smashing right through the door.
I was rid of him once and for all.

The very next night
when I turned out the light
and was ready to lay down my head,
I heard my kid brother
cry out to my mother,
"Hey, Ma, something's under my bed."

Joan Horton

Oh My Darling, Frankenstein

Oh my darling,
oh my darling,
oh my darling,
Frankenstein.
I abhor you
and adore you.
You're my darling,
Frankenstein.

Your creator
was a doctor
in a castle
near the Rhine.
On a slab
inside his lab
you were constructed,
Frankenstein.

Arms and legs and
head and torso,
that the doctor
did combine.
Bolts of lightning,
very frightening,
gave you life, dear
Frankenstein.

Then you rose up
from the table
with a bellow
and a whine.
You went lurching,
you were searching
for some dinner,
Frankenstein.

When the townsfolk
saw you coming,
you sent shivers
down their spines.
So they chased you
with their pitchforks
and their torches,
Frankenstein.

Then you lumbered
in the forest,
where you hid
amongst the pine
while the doc, he
did concoct me—
yes, a bride
for Frankenstein.

We were married
in the castle,
and forever
you'll be mine.
We're a creature
double feature,
oh my darling,
Frankenstein.

Kenn Nesbitt

Wedding Guest

A dragon walked into a room
where a joining of hearts was in bloom.
When the wedding was done
the dragon's the one
who toasted the bride and the groom.

Linda Knaus

As I Was Walking

As I was walking
out one day,
my head fell off
and rolled away.
I really do not
miss my head.
It doesn't bother me.
I'm dead.

Bruce Lansky

30

The Headless Horseman's Haircut

The headless horseman's hair was
getting scruffy 'round the ears.
He hadn't had a decent cut
in over twenty years.

He'd heard about a barber
who was recommended by
another headless horseman,
so he thought him worth a try.

He tied his horse outside the shop
on Second Avenue,
went in and asked the barber
for a shave and a shampoo.

He said, "I'd like my hair cut short,
but leave some length in back.
I'll need a dandruff treatment, too.
I'm fond of wearing black."

The headless horseman thought a bit
before instructing him,
"And then if time allows it, sir,
my moustache needs a trim."

He left there feeling confident
at quarter after one.
He turned and told the barber,
"I'll be back here when you're done."

Linda Knaus

Library of Congress Cataloging-in-Publication Data

Dinner with dracula : a spine-tingling collection of frighteningly funny poems / edited by Bruce Lansky; illustrated by Mike Gordon.
    p. cm.
    Summary: "A collection of spooky, funny poems about vampires, ghosts, Frankenstein, and other creatures"–Provided by publisher.
    ISBN 0-88166-512-6 (Meadowbrook Press) ISBN 0-689-05231-6 (Simon & Schuster)
    1. Supernatural–Juvenile poetry. 2. Monsters–Juvenile poetry. 3. Children's poetry, American. I. Lansky, Bruce. II. Gordon, Mike, ill.
    PS595.S94D56 2006
    811.008'037–dc22
                        2005020849

Editorial Director: Christine Zuchora-Walske
Coordinating Editor and Copyeditor: Angela Wiechmann
Proofreader: Alicia Ester
Production Manager: Paul Woods
Graphic Design Manager: Tamara Peterson
Illustrations and Cover Art: Mike & Carl Gordon

Published by Meadowbrook Press, 5451 Smetana Drive, Minnetonka, Minnesota 55343

www.meadowbrookpress.com

BOOK TRADE DISTRIBUTION by Simon and Schuster, a division of Simon and Schuster, Inc., 1230 Avenue of the Americas, New York, New York 10020

12 11 10 09 08 07 06   10 9 8 7 6 5 4 3 2 1

Printed in Malaysia

Credits

"Sweet Dreams" copyright © 1991 by Joyce Armor, previously published in *Kids Pick the Funniest Poems* (Meadowbrook Press); "The Creature" and "Frankenstein's Walk" copyright © 2006 by Bill Dodds; "Fraidy Cat" copyright © 2004 by Matthew M. Fredericks, previously published in *Rolling in the Aisles* (Meadowbrook Press); "Mama Monster's Lullaby" copyright © 2006 by Marilyn Helmer; "Hey, Ma, Something's under My Bed" copyright © 1998 by Joan Horton, previously published in *Miles of Smiles* (Meadowbrook Press); "My Gramps and I Are Werewolves!" copyright © 2006 by Kathy Kenney-Marshall; "The Headless Horseman's Haircut," "Wedding Guest," and "Which Witch?" copyright © 2006 by Linda Knaus; "As I Was Walking" copyright © 2000 by Bruce Lansky, previously published in *If Pigs Could Fly…And Other Deep Thoughts* (Meadowbrook Press); "Creepy Pizza," "Frankenswine," and "Vampire Brat" copyright © 2006 by Neal Levin; "Advice from Dracula" copyright © 2001 by Kenn Nesbitt, previously published in *The Aliens Have Landed at Our School!* (Meadowbrook Press); "Oh My Darling, Frankenstein" copyright © 2006 by Kenn Nesbitt, based on an idea by Max Nesbitt; "Science Homework" copyright © 2006 by Kenn Nesbitt; "The Fall-Apart Monster" copyright © 2006 by Eric Ode; "Bigfoot's Bottom" and "I Thought I Saw a Ghost Last Night" copyright © 2006 by Paul R. Orshoski; "Scary Costume" copyright © 2002 by Robert Pottle, previously published in *MOXIE DAY and Family*, used with permission from Blue Lobster Press; "The Creature in the Classroom" copyright © 1996 by Jack Prelutsky, previously published in *A Pizza the Size of the Sun*, used by permission of HarperCollins Publishers; "Tinkle, Tinkle, Little Bat" copyright © 2004 by Dianne Rowley, previously published in *Rolling in the Aisles* (Meadowbrook Press); "The Two-Headed Monster" copyright © 2006 by Darren Sardelli; and "Under the Bed" copyright © 2002 by Penny Trzynka. All poems used by permission of the authors or publishers.

Acknowledgments

Many thanks to the following teachers and their students who tested poems for this anthology:

Kathy Austrian, Lakeway Elementary, Austin, TX
Mark Benthall, Lakeway Elementary, Austin, TX
Cherie Birch, East Elementary, New Richmond, WI
David Burks, Cave Hill School, Eastbrook, ME
Diane Clapp, Lincoln Elementary, Faribault, MN
Niki Danou, Groveland Elementary, Minnetonka, MN
Jeremy Engebretson, Groveland Elementary, Minnetonka, MN
Elizabeth Erickson, East Elementary, New Richmond, WI
Pam Greer, East Elementary, New Richmond, WI
Jennifer Hahn, Groveland Elementary, Minnetonka, MN

Mary Jensen, East Elementary, New Richmond, WI
Kathy Kenney-Marshall, McCarthy Elementary, Framingham, MA
Carolyn Larsen, Rum River Elementary, Andover, MN
Hope Nadeau, East Elementary, New Richmond, WI
Mary Niermann, Lincoln Elementary, Faribault, MN
Mary Ellen Redden, Alexander Central School, Alexander, NY
Andrea Rutkowski, Miscoe Hill School, Mendon, MA
Suzanne Storbeck, Holy Name School, Wayzata, MN
Julie White, East Elementary, New Richmond, WI.